The Recurring Adventures of
Beau and Bailea

Rocky Angelette

ISBN 978-1-63903-255-6 (paperback)
ISBN 978-1-0980-1560-2 (hardcover)
ISBN 978-1-0980-1563-3 (digital)

Christian Faith Publishing, Inc.
832 Park Avenue
Meadville, PA 16335
www.christianfaithpublishing.com

Printed in the United States of America

To my son, Gabriel.

You remind me each and every day

The purpose that

GOD

Has for me.

Your imagination and your personality

Inspire me.

Your soft servant's heart

It consumes me.

Many adventures we shall go on.

Many worlds we will see.

Many mountains we will conquer.

Daddy loves ya, kid.

I couldn't be prouder.

What if I told you that the fastest duck in the tri-county area was on the brink of the greatest race he would *never* have to run? But what if I told you that all of this was destined to happen by way of an unfortunate event?

Hey, everyone! That's me, Beau. I am—well, I was—the fastest duck in the tri-county area and held that title for three years straight! There was no one out there who could come close to catching my tail feathers, much less beat me. I was a bolt of lightning!

Now, most athletes have their traditions after a win. For me, after I won a race, I found myself at a stretch of water near my farm that I call Champion Bay. There, I would admire my medal and myself in the reflection of the water. Boy, did we look good together too! But this was right when everything got all messed up. Or so I thought...

As I was paddling, there was a large gator not too far behind me, and he was creeping in slowly. I was clearly too distracted to notice. I mean who wouldn't be. Just then, I felt the rush of a mighty wave! At the same time, there dug into my feathers the talons of a large hawk! They were closing in from all angles. I was a goner, as far as I was concerned.

But then I realized that the hawk was on a rescue mission when I heard him say, "Time to get you out of here, Beau!" At this point, I was feeling a bit relieved when all of a sudden…SNAP!!

Somewhere, moments later…

When I woke up I heard a voice say, "Well done, Commander," followed by a loud "Helloooooo, Beau!" Now I was face to face with a very loud goat. "I'm Sir Billiam! I'm one of the gatekeepers in heaven, and I keep the shift here from four until eleven. You may notice that people up here speak with a flow but that's one of the perks that comes with the halo. Bustin' rhymes all the time at the drop of a dime!" Though Sir Billiam assured me I was still alive, I couldn't help but ask, "But if I'm still alive, why am I here in heaven and crutches? This was going to take some getting used to. I've never moved this slowly before," I said to Sir Billiam. I couldn't believe this was happening to me. However, as upsetting as this was, I couldn't help but wonder what was beyond the gate. "Could I take a look?" I then asked Sir Billiam. "Why of course you can! That was already part of the plan, my man," he said.

8

"Hey, what's going on?" I asked Sir Billiam.

"Oh, you aren't going to need these anymore. When you're beyond the gates, you're fully restored!" he assured me.

"Now that's what I'm talking about. Let me go show these animals that these clouds haven't seen a bolt of lightning quite like me!" I said excitedly.

Sir Billiam and I stood at the gates, and
I was astonished at what I saw. I never saw

so many animals having so much fun without a
care in the world. It truly was heaven.

12

As we got a little farther down, we approached this large cow fussing some cats for trying to take some of her milk. "Holy cow!" I said.

"Little ducky, that's exactly what I am. A holy cow is what they call me, but you can just call me ma'am! Actually, the name is MooMomma and don't mind if I sing. We all have our talents, and hitting high notes is my thing—la la laaaaaa!"

"I'll take it from here Billy so you can go on back to your gate because Beau here has an appointment, and we definitely don't want to be late," said Moo-Momma.

Moo-Momma then told me how Papa Bear was going to be excited to see me! "Papa Bear? Papa Bear wants to see me? How exciting!" I knew that if there was anyone who could tell me why I was here, it would be Him.

As Moo-Momma and I reached the top of the large hill we were now face to face with a large cave. I then ask Moo-Momma, "What's He like?"

With a huge smile on her face, she took it away: "Papa has very good hearing, which has allowed Him to hear every word you've said. So remember that next time you're saying your prayers just before bed. Call as you need without a second guess in mind and know that He's never late but always on time. His sight is magnificent, so He never misses all the good that you do. In fact, He was there the very first time that you flew. He's a very mighty Papa: the strongest that anyone has ever known. He can move the mightiest of mountains, so you can always find your way back home. He gives the greatest hugs, and He comforts you when you're down. And that's what He is doing when you claim that He's not around. He's known to have great digging skills to dig dens for Him to live, but dwelling inside your heart is what His character truly intends. So don't ever worry about the love that He has inside, for His love for you is as big as the universe is wide."

16

17

Just as Moo-Momma finished she let out a loud, "Hey, Papa-B, you in there?" I could now feel His large footsteps heading our way—boom, boom, boom! As Papa Bear walked out of the cave, I felt excitement like I've never felt before. He was mighty just as she said. I bet He really could move a mountain!

At this point, I couldn't help myself as I dashed toward Papa! He then tossed me on His shoulder. "Boy oh boy, have I ever looked forward to this exact day. Come Beau, you have much to ask but I have so much more to say."

As we made our way into a trail, we found ourselves deep into a large forest. And I mean large! The trees were enormous. Far bigger than any tree back home. Everything was huge, even the flowers!

During our walk, we came to a stopping place, and Papa began to give me the answers that I was searching for. He told me that though I was given a gift to be a fast runner, winning medals was just a small part of why He created me.

He told me that there were so many animals on earth that needed help and was in need of a hero! "Like you," He told me. Me, a hero? I've never been called that before.

"So why create me to be fast if being a hero would have nothing to do with that?" I asked.

He then showed me something that I had never realized about myself. "Remember your first race? You weren't always as fast as you are now. In fact, you were pretty slow, and you ended up in last place," He said. "Winning races didn't always come this easy, but it was your courage and hard-work that made it this breezy. It was never about how fast you ran with your shoes but everything to do with the courage that pushed you to never lose."

He was right. I let all this winning get to my head, and I had forgotten how slow I use to be. But it took Him to slow me down and open up my eyes to give me the answers as to why I was up here.

I now realize that Papa Bear's reasons far exceeded my talents. It had more to do with my courage than anything else.

Papa then reminded me that He wasn't far should I ever need Him as He put a chain around my neck with a key on the end. "Here Beau, you're going to need this so you can get on your way. Now go and do what hero's do and save the day," Papa said.

"Commander Buxley will take you exactly where you need to be. I promise that the best is yet to come, Beau. Just you wait and see. This is all going to make sense very soon. If you just hold on to your courage, then the limit will be the moon," Papa assured me.

"Wait, aren't you the same commander who saved me from the gator?" I asked.

He just nodded.

"Why in the world would you want to change into a hawk? Dogs are much more fun. Hawks are scary-looking!" I asked.

"It helped you out that day didn't it, but I change when it's necessary. So I wouldn't be so worried about hawks and how they look scary," he responded.

Before I knew it, we arrived at the edge of a pretty tall cliff. When we looked down, I couldn't believe my eyes. There were dogs everywhere! "So you'll need a rider because of your leg, and I know just the one that I won't have to beg." said Commander.

"Bailea, COOOOOME!" he shouted.

Out of all the dogs in the field, only one head popped up! It was Bailea. In a split second, she came flying toward us and knocked down about ten other dogs in the process. She was coming in hot! Commander informed me that Bailea used to be a hunting dog— which, being a duck, was of no good news to me at all! But given I'm a runner, I decided to do just that but she still managed to catch up with me. Bailey was fast as well!

"Hi, I'm BAILEA! How are you? I'm fine, thanks for asking! No, wait! I'm great! Great, great, great! Can we start? Huh? Huh? You must be Beau. You look like a Beau! Has anyone ever told you that? You must get it all the time, don't you! Gosh you're fast! Did you know that about yourself? I'm fast too! See?" Bailea could hardly contain herself.

"Yyyyyyyyyes!" Bailea shouted as she took off toward the gate.

Before she could go any further, Commander caught up and stopped her in her tracks! "Bailea, you cut this out right now and act like a pro. We've got work to do, so you can't be acting this way before you go!" Commander shouted.

At that moment, an owl swooped down and addressed Commander Buxley, "Commander, what could possibly be so serious that you felt the need to snap? You know that around this time of day I'm busy taking my afternoon nap!

Oh wait, this must be the duck I was hearing about earlier this week! Buh…buh…Beau? That's it! I'm so excited I could barely get it out my beak!"

"Who are you?" I asked the owl.

"Well, my name is Hugo, and if Commander failed to say, I'll be an extra help for you as you go along your way. When wisdom is what you need, wisdom is what you'll receive. Therefore, there's no need to worry because wisdom helps you believe. So when you're at your wit's end, just give out a whooo! Come on, give a try you two!"

"Whooooo!" Beau and Bailea yelled together.

"There you go, you two! What a who that you two blew reveals that it's true that this journey is meant for you! I'll come flying by to tend to your request, for no who is too small to keep me in my nest. At the sound of any who, time will stop while I'm in midflight. But not to worry because within seconds, I'll be within your sights. I bid you a safe journey, and I'll be there for any little peep. But excuse me, my new friends, I have to go and get some sleep." Hugo then flew up and back into his nest.

After meeting Hugo, we made our way to the gate where Sir Billiam and Moo-Momma would be waiting for us. Apparently, it was time to go.

When we arrived at the gate, it began to open up, and that's when I remembered what would happen to my leg. It would go back to being injured once I walked on through. I wasn't looking forward to that at all. I was enjoying my time up here, but I knew that I had to press on if I was to proceed with these heroic missions that Papa Bear talked to me about.

So with Sir Billiam's help, I hopped up on Bailea's back, and he secured my crutch on her side.

Just then, Bailea's halo slowly slid down toward me in the position of a steering wheel. "What's this for?" I asked. Commander then explained that this was going to be the way that we would get transported from mission to mission. "All you have to do is insert the key, turn to the right and watch and see. All over the world you two will travel as the missions before you will soon unravel. Good luck to you both and I'll be seeing you two soon. Be sure to hold on tight Beau, for once that button is pushed, you're bound to go...

More excited than I could contain, I accidentally hit the ZOOP button, and immediately Bailea and I disappeared into thin air! I don't think that was supposed to happen. Not yet at least. Gosh, I hope he wasn't about to tell us something important.

Seconds later, I woke up from my sleep. I was back home. It was dark, and everything was as it was right after the alligator accident. Was it all one big dream? I was so upset. The cast was still on my foot, but no key was to be found around my neck. And what about everyone that I met? Sir Billiam, Commander Buxley, Moo-Momma, Papa Bear, Hugo and…

40

"Good morning, Beau!" a shout came, which sent me flying for what felt like miles in the air. I was so frightened until I noticed that it was Bailea! And not only was it Bailea, but she had the key around her neck. This really did happen! "You ready to go?" Bailea asked.

"Is this even a question? I was born for this," I replied as I took off as fast as I could toward Bailea, letting out some loud quacks!

Hoby sits up in bed trying to make sense of his dream. He doesn't see how he could be much of a hero given his season ending injury. However, Hoby still has the feeling that someone, somewhere, is trying to tell him something...but what or who could it be? What do you think?

"Wow, look at this! But how… how is this possible?"

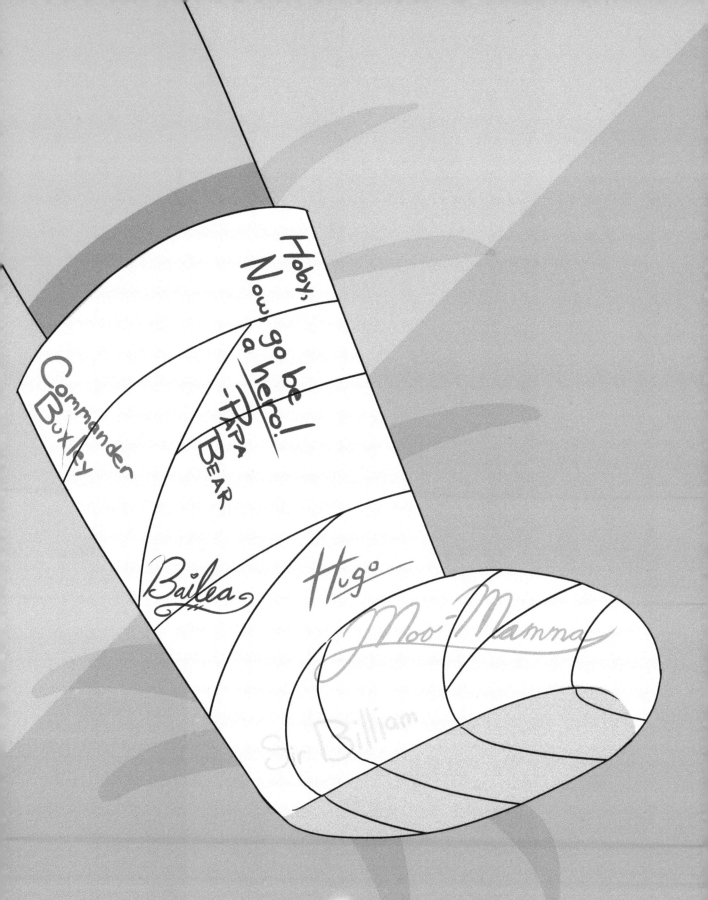

About the Author

As far back as his mind can take him, Rocky Angelette can still remember a small boy lying in bed and staying up about an extra hour and a half past his bedtime listening to his Walkman before officially calling it a night. With headphones on and shut off from the world while his parents thought he was asleep, he was creating. His imagination would take off to the beat of whatever song he was listening to, and an entire world of characters and a story line would begin to unfold. That was nearly twenty-five years ago, and to this day, he still finds himself arbitrarily creating stories in his mind from the seemingly normal lives going on around him. Finally, after many years of creating that have gone by, he is finally making his dreams a reality.

The Bible says that we are made in His image, and the God that he knows is a very creative God. He has blessed us all with specific gifts and talents and passions. Though Rocky's other talents were obvious to the naked eye, his passions went unseen. Athletics were a dominating force in his family, but creating and telling stories seemed to hold much more weight. God placed this desire inside of him for a reason, for a calling. He calls us to reach the nations, and He did so with words written on several pages. Rocky's prayer is that his stories will do the same as the Bible did: inspire, encourage, and comfort.

May God bless you beyond your wildest imagination!

Printed in the USA
CPSIA information can be obtained
at www.ICGtesting.com
LVHW061251211123
764112LV00014B/669